LITTLE BEE'S DAY IN THE GARDEN

BY SHANNON L MOKRY

Have I not commanded you? Be strong and courageous. Do not be frightened, and do not be dismayed, for the Lord your God is with you wherever you go." - Joshua 1:9

Today, Little Bee was heading out of the hive for the first time.

"Just follow us," the other bees said.

"It's beautiful in the garden!" they encouraged her.

Little Bee wasn't so sure.

The world outside was different, strange, and...

SCARY!

Inside the hive was safe.

Little Bee was afraid, but she did not want to let fear control her.

So, Little Bee took a deep breath.

Then, she took another and launched herself from the hive.

She had done it!

The world was big, bright, and full of color.

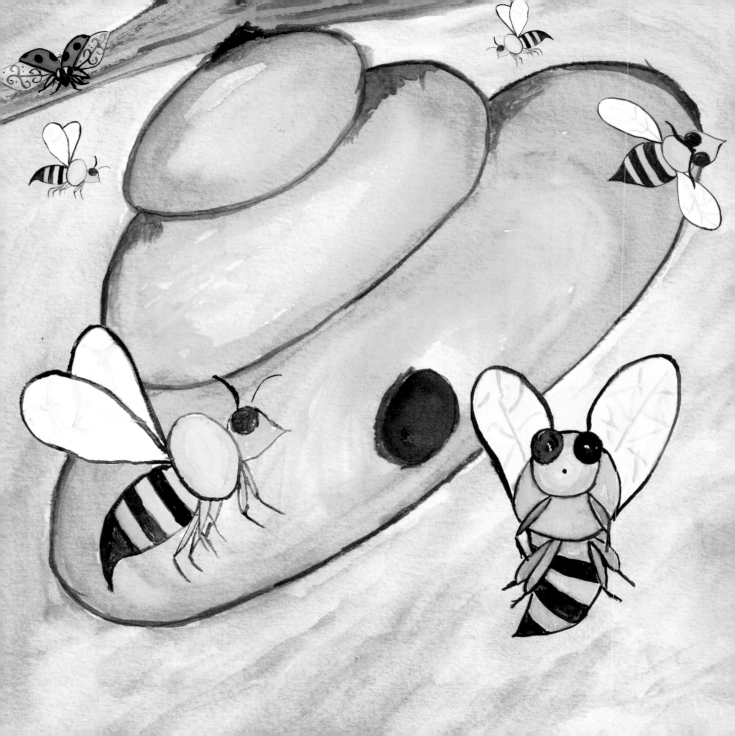

one of her friends flew over to encourage her. "Pick your favorite color and we will go see if you like what you find," her friend said.

A cluster of flowers reminded her of the inside
of the hive.
The flowers were all yellow and orange.
They smelled wonderful, so they flew closer.

Another bee joined them, but it looked and
smelled different.
Little Bee was confused.
The new bee had a green head and body with
the same yellow and black striped back.
"Hello," Little Bee greeted this new bee, hoping to
make a new friend.

Her friend giggled. "That is a sweat bee. She has a one track mind and no hive."

"No hive?" Little Bee asked in shock.

"Nope, so they are focused on finding food."

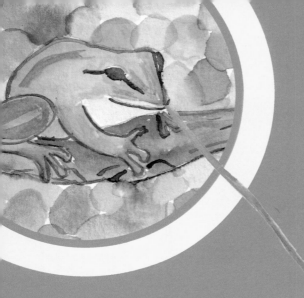

Something green moved and caught her eye.
A frog shot out his tongue and caught some
lunch.
"That is a tree frog," her friend told her. "Don't
worry, they don't eat bees."

Next, she saw some giant flowers aimed at the sun.

"What is that?" whispered Little Bee.

"The sun flower or the bumble bee?" her friend whispered back.

"Both, but now I know." Little Bee flew past the sunflowers.

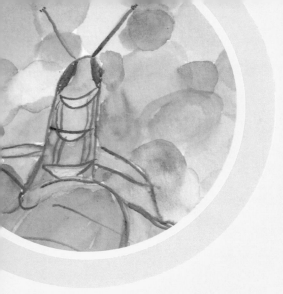

They flew into an open space and looked around.
Another small green creature jumped into view.
This time it was being chased.
"A cat—it looks like it is trying to catch a
grasshopper." Her friend buzzed away
uninterested.
Little Bee circled again to watch until the cat's tail
came a little too close to her.

Some bright pink flowers in the distance caught her eye.

The flowers were orchids and around them flew a strange blue insect.

"That is a blue orchid bee. Blue orchid bees only like orchids," Little Bee was told.

"That is a bee?" she wondered in amazement.

The world was a very big place full of all sorts
of wonderful things.
As she flew home that night, she was tired and
happy.
She had seen sweat bees, bumble bees, a frog,
a cat, grasshoppers, and orchid bees!
Little Bee had taken a leap of faith and it had
been amazing.

About the Author

Shannon L. Mokry grew up in sunny California. She now makes her home in Texas. She lives there with her husband, three daughters, two cats, one dog, and four chickens. In recent years she has taken on the role of homeschooling all three of her girls. The Bubbles stories were inspired by the stories she would tell her youngest daughter, Charlotte.

Some Bee Facts
extra information about the bees in the book

Honey Bee: The number one most common bee type. This is also the best-known bee type. Generally yellow with black stripes. They can sting but will usually leave you alone if you leave them alone. They live in a hive.

Sweat Bee: Attracted to Human Sweat, they eat nectar and pollen like other bees. They come in many different colors. Usually they have yellow faces, but can be a variety of colors on their bodies: green, brown, black, metallic or red. They are small bees often mistaken as small flies.

Bumble Bee: Large fuzzy bees. Mostly yellow and black, but can sometimes be mostly black. They make a loud buzz. Some are very endangered. They are social bees and live in a hive, although much smaller than a honey bee hive.

Orchid Bee: Usually rainforest bees, they have recently been found more and more in the United States. They come in many jewel colors, including green, brilliant blue, purple, red, gold, brassy, or a mixture of these colors. They are mostly attracted to orchids.

More books in this series
by Shannon L. Mokry

www.hyperurl.co/Little
PinkElephant

www.smarturl.it/
PurplePorcupine

www.smarturl.it/
YellowLlama

https://smarturl.it/blue
flamingo

www.smarturl.it/
SlothandSnail

www.smarturl.it/
LittlePandWDYS

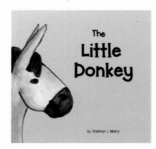

https://smarturl.it/Little
Donkey

https://smarturl.it/mouse
andpinkelephant

Other books by Shannon L. Mokry

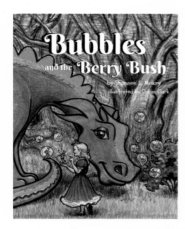

www.hyperurl.co/
BubblesBerryBush

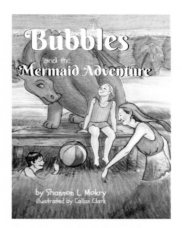

www.smarturl.it/
BubblesMermaid

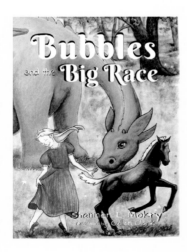

www.smarturl.it/
BubblesBigRace

www.smarturl.it/
TakeAWalkontheBeach

Books for Older Kids
by Shannon L. Mokry

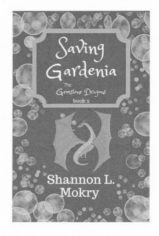

www.hyperurl.co/
EscapingGardenia

www.smarturl.it/
SavingGardenia

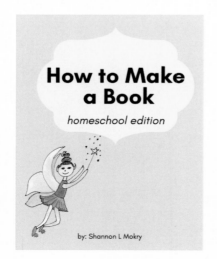

https://smarturl.it/
howtomakeabook

Lightning Source UK Ltd.
Milton Keynes UK
UKRC032042310322
400930UK00002B/15

9 781951 521455